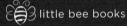 little bee books

251 Park Avenue South, New York, NY 10010
Copyright © 2020 by Little Bee Books
All rights reserved, including the right of reproduction in whole or
in part in any form.
Library of Congress Cataloging-in-Publication Data
is available upon request.
Printed in China TPL 0220
ISBN 978-1-4998-1003-5 (hardcover)
First Edition 10 9 8 7 6 5 4 3 2 1
ISBN 978-1-4998-1002-8 (paperback)
First Edition 10 9 8 7 6 5 4 3 2 1
ISBN 978-1-4998-1004-2 (ebook)

littlebeebooks.com

For more information about special discounts on bulk purchases,
please contact Little Bee Books at sales@littlebeebooks.com.

ALIEN NEXT DOOR

A NEW PLANET

by A. I. Newton
illustrated by Anjan Sarkar

little bee books

TABLE OF CONTENTS

BOUND FOR TRAGAS

HARRIS WALKER AND HIS BEST friend Roxy Martinez crouched in a cramped, dark storage container. They were hiding in the engine room of a spaceship zooming away from Earth to a distant planet known as Tragas. It had been a week since the ship took off.

A few months earlier, the two friends had met Zeke. Zeke and his parents were actually aliens from the planet Tragas. Zeke's parents traveled from planet to planet, studying the culture of each one's residents.

When Zeke arrived on Earth, Harris tried hard to prove that Zeke was an alien. But once Zeke told him the truth, he and Harris quickly became good friends and Harris did his best to protect Zeke's secret. Although Roxy didn't know the truth about Zeke, they had become good friends, too.

But when the time came for Zeke and his parents to return to Tragas, Harris told Roxy about Zeke's secret. To prove it, he and Roxy snuck onto the spaceship that would take the aliens home.

Which is exactly when Zeke and his family got on board and blasted off.

When Zeke discovered that his Earth friends were on the ship, he asked them if they wanted his parents to turn the ship around and bring them home.

"After all I've heard about Tragas," Harris said to Zeke, "I don't want to give up my chance to see your home planet."

"And I still can't believe that you're an alien!" Roxy said. "Harris knew all along, but I didn't believe him."

And so now Harris and Roxy hunkered down, listening to the low hum of the ship's engines.

"How long do we have stay inside this thing?" Harris asked.

"All the way to Tragas," Roxy replied.

"I know I said that I really wanted to see Tragas, but I'm really getting bored," said Harris.

At that moment, the doors to the storage unit swung open, and there stood Zeke. During his time on Earth, Zeke shape-shifted his appearance to look like a human.

But once he got onto the ship, he changed back to his true Tragas form, a blob-like creature with speckled green skin, five eyes, and six tentacles extending from his shoulders.

He hovered above the floor and put on his translation glasses, which helped translate Tragonian to the language of any planet Zeke and his parents visited.

"I still can't get used to your real form," Harris said, stepping out and stretching.

"Well, I'm pretty used to your human form," Zeke replied, laughing. "And believe me, humans looked pretty weird to me when I first landed on Earth."

Zeke reached into his pocket and pulled out a handful of shiny purple slugs and striped leaves. "Here, I brought you these kreslars and some pritchiks for lunch," Zeke said. His hands started glowing, and the food cooked, turning crispy.

"These are weird," Harris complained, crunching down on a pritchik leaf.

"Really? Everyone loves them on Tragas," Zeke said, popping a couple into his mouth. "And wait until you see the trees they grow on!"

Roxy and Harris munched on the leaves.

"I am sorry that we have no Earth food on board," Zeke said. "But we didn't know you'd be joining us."

"I know. I don't mean to complain," Harris said. "And I'm really excited to see Tragas. How much longer before we get there?"

"About a week," Zeke said.

Harris and Roxy groaned.

"So I wanted to ask you," said Harris, "how come we're not—you know—floating, like astronauts on space missions?"

"The Barzium crystals that power this ship also create an artificial gravity field on board," Zeke explained.

"Cool!" said Roxy.

"Zekelabraxis!" came a shout from Zeke's father, over the ship-wide intercom system. He was using Zeke's real, Tragonian name. "Where have you disappeared to now?"

2 SNEAKING OUT

ZEKE TOOK OFF HIS TRANSLATION glasses and rushed from the engine room. Hovering above the floor, he sped through the narrow, twisting hallways of the ship.

He arrived at the ship's bridge out of breath. His parents sat at control panels piloting the spacecraft.

"You have been vanishing for long periods of time ever since we left Earth," Xad, his father, said.

"Yes, Zekelabraxis," his mother, Quar, added. "Where do you go?"

"Um, well, I—" Zeke stammered, "I was checking on the Barzium crystals."

Xad checked a readout on his panel. "They are fine," he said.

Zeke nodded. But he started to worry that he couldn't keep the fact that his friends were on board a secret for much longer.

Back in the engine room, Harris and Roxy peeked out of the storage container. Seeing that no one was around, they stepped out.

"I'm happy to be out of that box," said Harris. "I can't wait until we get to Tragas."

"Why don't we play a game to pass the time?" Roxy suggested. "How about I spy?"

Harris shrugged. *Anything to relieve the boredom.*

"Okay, I'll go first," Roxy said, looking around the engine room. "I spy with my little eye, um . . . a tall, black, blinky, spinning . . . uh, thing. . . ."

Harris raised his eyebrows.

"This is not going to work, is it?" Roxy admitted. "How can we play this game when we don't what any of this alien stuff is?"

"I'm hungry," said Harris.

"You're always hungry," Roxy sighed.

"There's got to be something better than slugs and leaves to eat on this ship," Harris said. "And I'm going to find it!" He headed for the door leading out of the engine room.

"But you don't know where you're going!" Roxy said. She shook her head but joined him, not wanting them to be separated.

They snuck quietly down a hallway, looking for the food storage area.

"I think the kitchen is in here," said Harris, walking through a dark doorway.

As they entered the room, Harris and Roxy found themselves in a giant hall. They were standing on the ship's bridge! Flashing control panels lined the room. A huge window looked out on the stars zipping past them.

"This is not the kitchen, Harris!" Roxy whispered. "We're lucky Zeke's parents aren't on the bridge. Let's get out of here."

Harris and Roxy turned to leave, and crashed right into the big, green, tentacled Tragonian form of Xad!

"Plixnar zabondigrit!" exclaimed Xad in Tragonian.

3

EXPOSED

XAD SLIPPED ON A PAIR OF translation glasses.

"Harris! Roxy!" he cried. "Why are you on our ship? Does Zeke know you are here?"

"Yes, Xad," Zeke said, rushing into the room. "I do know."

Quar joined the group.

"What is going on here? Harris? Roxy? What are you doing here?" she asked.

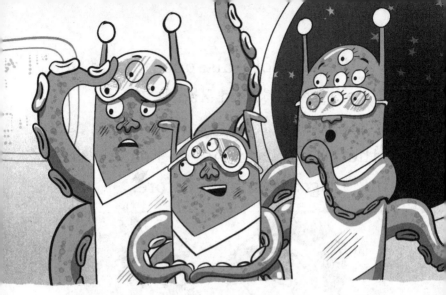

"I discovered them just after the ship took off from Earth," Zeke explained.

"I'm sorry," Harris said. "I wanted to show Roxy the truth about Zeke once I knew he was leaving. She didn't believe me, so I brought her onto the ship as proof. Zeke had shown it to me the day before. But then we got trapped when you all boarded."

"We are both disappointed in you, Zekelabraxis," said Xad.

Harris and Roxy looked at each other. They had never heard Zeke's full Tragonian name before.

"Yes," agreed Quar. "First, that you told Harris the truth about being from Tragas."

"But he was being punished for lying to his parents when he was just telling the truth," Zeke said. "I couldn't let that happen."

Quar sighed. "I'm glad you were being a good friend, Zeke. But this now puts us all in a difficult position."

Xad pressed a button on a control panel, calling up the ship's fuel gauge.

"Hmm . . . we do not have enough fuel to turn around, return Harris and Roxy to Earth, and still make it back to Tragas. We are going to have to refuel on Tragas in order to get Harris and Roxy home."

"Well, it looks like you guys will be seeing Tragas after all!" Zeke said excitedly.

"Zekelabraxis, I do not think you are taking this situation seriously enough!" Xad said sternly.

"This is all my fault," said Harris. "Please don't be mad at Zeke."

"We'll do our best to not get in the way," Roxy added.

"Have you thought about your parents?" Quar asked. "Don't you think they'll be worried?"

Harris and Roxy both froze. They had been so caught up in this amazing adventure, they hadn't thought about their parents.

"I was supposed to be home for dinner in an hour!" cried Roxy. "But that was like a week ago!"

"I'm supposed to go bowling with my parents tonight!" says Harris. "I mean, the night we left."

Roxy looked at Harris.

"What are we going to do?" she asked.

4

A WAY OUT . . . MAYBE

XAD PLACED HIS FINGERTIPS ON either side of his head and mind-projected a star chart from the ship's main computer onto the ceiling.

"There may be a way to solve this problem," he said. "But I won't know for sure if my calculations are correct until we reach Tragas."

A few minutes later, Harris and Roxy joined Zeke on the bridge. Though they remained concerned about their parents, they were amazed by what they saw out the ship's main window.

Flaming yellow stars, icy blue planets, and multicolored nebulae swirled past them in a brilliant moving painting.

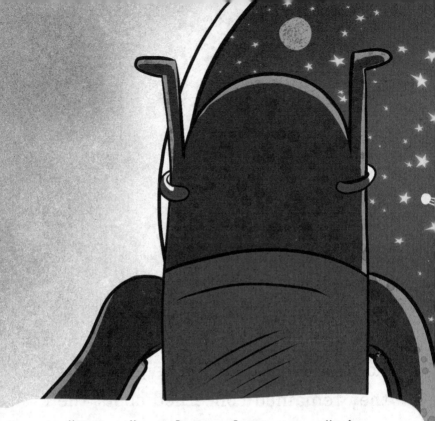

"Wow!" exclaimed Harris. "It's so weird and beautiful at the same time. I thought I knew what space would look like from watching movies and reading comic books, but this is beyond anything I could have imagined."

"And I would never have imagined in a million years that I would ever be traveling through space!" Roxy added. "So what's Tragas like, Zeke—elix, uh . . . ?"

"You can still just call me Zeke," he replied. "At least until we land on Tragas."

The three friends laughed.

"Well, Tragas looks really different than Earth," Zeke explained. "Our lakes are yellow. Waterfalls flow up, not down. And some of the trees are striped."

Harris's face turned serious. "Remember you told me about the Kraka Beast?" he asked.

"Yes, it eats trees and buildings, and can destroy an entire city!" Zeke said.

"Sounds dangerous," said Roxy.

Zeke pulled out a helmet and slipped it onto his head. "This is an encyclo-helmet. It will show me what season it is right now on Tragas."

He pressed a switch on the helmet, and suddenly, flowers of all colors bloomed all around them. Three-headed purple birds flew through the air. Striped trees full of orange leaves rustled in the soft breeze.

"Don't worry, it's summer on Tragas," Zeke said as he turned the helmet off. "And the Kraka Beast always hibernates in summer."

Xad floated into the room and handed glowing metal rings to Harris and Roxy.

"Rest these on your head," he said.

"Like a crown?" Roxy asked.

"Correct," said Xad.

Harris and Roxy placed the rings onto their heads. Right before Zeke's five eyes, they both transformed into Tragonians!

They now had green skin and floated off the ground. Harris had five eyes and six tentacles, while Roxy had seven eyes and four tentacles.

"Wow!" said Zeke.

"What?" asked Harris.

Xad pressed a button near the window, and the glass changed into a mirror.

"'Wow' is right!" said Roxy, seeing her reflection. She looked over at Harris. "You look, um, like Zeke!"

"This is just a mind projection illusion," Xad explained. "These transformo-rings project the image of a Tragonian body into the minds of anyone looking at you so that no one will know you're from Earth."

"This is so cool!," said Harris.

"Really? They feel warm to me," said Xad. Harris, Roxy, and Zeke all started laughing.

"Anyway, these rings will also act like our translation glasses," Xad continued. "You will be able to understand Tragonians, and they will be able to understand you."

"Tragas, here we come!" said Harris, wigging his tentacles.

THE FINAL FEW DAYS OF THE journey to Tragas were much more enjoyable now that Harris and Roxy no longer had to hide.

"I'm glad we can finally walk around. This ship is so cool!" said Harris, watching Zeke adjust controls on the bridge.

"Everything about it is amazing!" said Roxy.

"Well, except the food. But I don't mind it as much now," said Harris, popping a squishy yellow blob into his mouth.

BEEP! BEEP! BEEP!

An alarm sounded suddenly.

"Is something wrong?" Roxy asked.

"No," replied Xad. "That is the signal that we are approaching Tragas."

Harris, Roxy, and Zeke stared out the window. A small orange-and-green dot grew larger and larger.

"There it is!" cried Zeke. "My home!"

A few minutes later, the colorful surface of Tragas filled the window.

"Take your seats everyone," said Quar. "Prepare for landing."

The ship drifted through purple clouds. A few minutes later, they landed at the Tragas spaceport.

Xad looked at Harris and Roxy.

"Now remember," he said. "You must keep the transformo-rings on your heads. If anyone discovers that we brought you here from Earth, Quar and I would certainly lose our jobs. It will take two days to refuel the ship. You must make everyone believe that you are Tragonians for the entire time you are here"

Harris and Roxy nodded and slipped the rings back onto their heads.

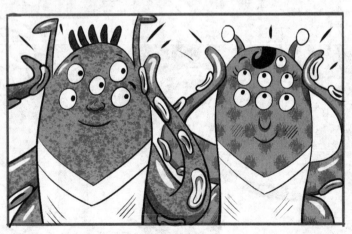

Everyone left the ship. Xad and Quar went to the Tragas Cultural Council to file their report on Earth.

"Come on," said Zeke. "I'll show you around."

As they walked from the spaceport, Harris and Roxy were amazed by everything they saw.

"Wow, the water in that lake really is yellow," Harris said, pointing.

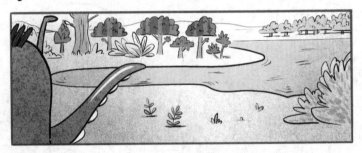

"And look at the waterfall!" cried Roxy. "How can the water flow up?!"

"Waterfalls on Tragas create a reverse gravitational field," explained Zeke.

"Check out the striped tree," said Harris. "Even the leaves are striped."

"That's the pritchik tree," said Zeke, pulling off one of its leaves. "We ate some the leaves on the ship. Hungry?" Zeke offered the leaf to Harris.

"No thanks," Harris said.

"There's so much to see and so little time," said Roxy.

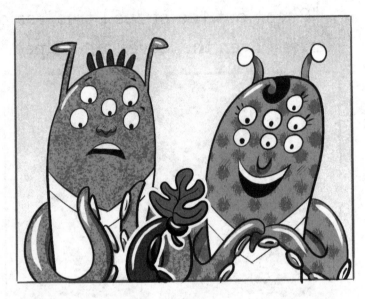

"Hey, I have an idea," said Zeke. "Let's rent some zumda cycles. They move pretty quickly, and we can see more of Tragas. There's a rental shop right around the corner."

Harris and Roxy followed Zeke. Suddenly, a huge, hairy beast came barreling around the corner, heading right for them.

"Look out!" cried Harris. "It's a monster!"

6

OUT ON THE TOWN

HARRIS BACKED AWAY IN FEAR. Roxy lifted her arms in defense and was shocked at the sight of her own tentacles.

Zeke opened *his* tentacles wide. The charging creature ran right up to him and licked his face.

"That's a mouse!" Harris said.

"A really, really *big* mouse!" added Roxy. "It's as big as a dog."

"And just as friendly!" said Zeke, scratching the top of the mouse's head. The mouse trotted off happily. "They're all over Tragas."

"Weird," said Harris.

"Not any weirder than keeping a tiny mouse in a cage as a pet on Earth," Zeke pointed out.

A few minutes later, they arrived at the zumda cycle rental shop. A row of sleek-looking cycles sat in a line.

"Um, Zeke, we don't have any Tragonian money," said Roxy. "How will we pay for this?"

"Yeah, I only have a dollar eighty-five in Earth money in my pocket," Harris said, looking down at his long green body. "But I can't even see my pockets anymore!"

"Oh, we don't have to carry money on Tragas," Zeke explained. "Everything is kept in a central account. Watch."

Zeke extended one of his tentacles. The owner of the zumda rental shop reached out with one of his. The two tentacles touched, and a jagged red electrical current sizzled between them.

"Thank you," said the rental man. "Enjoy yourselves and be safe."

Zeke turned to his friends. "Pick a cycle and climb on board!"

"Wait!" whispered Roxy, looking confused. "There are no pedals. How do we make this thing go?"

"Use your mind," Zeke said softly, lifting his fingers to his forehead. "The transformo-ring will do the rest."

Harris shook his head. Anyone watching saw his five eyeballs bounce back and forth around his head. "I'll give it a try."

He and Roxy each thought about their zumda cycles moving. The cycles took off, speeding down the road.

"Woo-hoo!" Harris cried. "This is the coolest bike ever!"

The three friends zoomed along the streets.

"What's that?" Roxy asked, pointing at a huge statue that circled through the air above a park. The statue had eleven eyes and ten arms.

"That's the great Tragaslovox," Zeke explained. "The founder of Tragas and the greatest Tragonian of all time."

They sped around a bend.

"Over there!" Zeke shouted above the roar of the zumda cycles' engines. "That's the house I used to live in."

Harris glanced at the building.

"How did you live in a house with curved walls and floors?" he asked.

"When you hover above the ground instead of walking, the shapes of rooms don't really matter," Zeke explained.

Harris nodded. *Makes as much sense as anything else I've seen here.*

Zeke spotted a hovering food truck.

"I'm starving," he said. "Let's get some gardash strands!"

The kids screeched to a stop and pulled up to the truck. Everyone got a steaming bowl of gardash strands— long, noodle-like purple strings.

The woman in the food truck reached her tentacle out toward Harris, who had a purple strand dangling from his mouth. He panicked.

She wants me to pay by touching tentacles. But I don't really have any tentacles!

"My treat!" said Zeke, seeing the situation and stepping up. Again, a jagged red electrical current passed between the two tentacles.

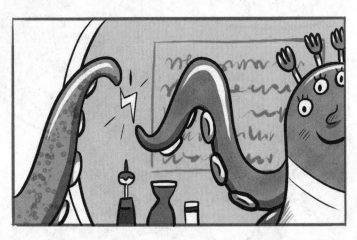

"Those gardash strands made me thirsty," Harris said when they finished eating. "I could use something to drink."

"I know just the place!" said Zeke. "Follow me!"

7

FACTORY TOUR

WITH ZEKE LEADING THE WAY, the three friends sped through the streets of Tragas.

"What's that?" asked Harris, pointing at a round, egg-shaped stadium in the sky.

"That is the main Bonkas arena," explained Zeke. "You remember, Bonkas is the official sport of Tragas. It's something like baseball on Earth, only it's played with thin sticks and ten balls."

"Maybe we could see a match?" Roxy suggested.

Zeke glanced up at the gigantic flashing sign that hovered in front of the stadium. It read:

"We're in luck, look!" said Zeke.

Harris and Roxy looked up at the sign, confused.

"Um . . . what does it say?" Harris asked his friend.

Zeke laughed.

"Sorry, I forgot for a moment that, although your transformo-rings translate speech, they don't translate writing, like translation glasses do," he said. "The sign says that there is a match tomorrow afternoon!"

"Cool!" said Roxy. "Why don't we all plan to go?"

A short time later, the three friends arrived at a large building that looked like a giant machine.

Huge gears and wheels spun. Brilliant lights of many colors flashed, and sounds blasted from long pipes sticking out of the building's roof.

"Wow!" said Roxy. "It's like a giant toy or a merry-go-round. What is it?"

"It's the factory where they make Saurlic, the most popular beverage on Tragas," Zeke explained.

"I tried it when your parents came to my house for dinner," Harris said to Zeke. "It's pretty good. It tastes like a cross between orange juice and lemonade."

"I remember it," said Roxy. "Yum!"

They hopped from their zumda cycles and onto a moving conveyor belt, joining Tragonians and other aliens on the tour. The belt took them past the various steps used to make Saurlic.

"In this step, dweelop are taken and crushed to release their juice," said a voice coming over a loudspeaker.

Harris watched as large green fruits with bumps all over their skin dropped into a spinning metal bin.

"I remember when you stuffed one of those into your mouth at lunch," he said to Zeke.

From a small hole at the bottom of the spinning bin, light green juice sprayed into a trench.

"Next," said the voice, "we add plenty of fresh water."

Spouts poured yellow lake water into the racing green juice, mixing them together.

"And now, the sweetness crystals," added the voice.

An avalanche of orange crystals poured into the moving liquid.

At the end of the trench, the mixture dropped into a huge funnel.

Finally, it dripped out the other end of a series of tubes as smooth orange-and-green liquid, which filled fancy bottles.

The moving belt dropped the visitors off at a long, narrow table, where everyone was treated to a free sample.

Harris gulped down his Saurlic. "This stuff is great!" he said, placing his empty glass on the table. Then he watched in amazement as the glass automatically refilled itself.

Following the tour, Harris, Roxy, and Zeke returned their zumda cycles and headed to Zeke's house for dinner.

At the dinner table, they took their transformo-rings off for the night. Harris struggled to figure out the best way to eat a long, clear zilnit rod. It crunched in his mouth as he chewed.

Harris watched as Zeke and his parents placed their zilnit rods into their mouths and absorbed them through their cheeks.

"What are your plans for tomorrow?" Xad asked.

"We're seeing a Bonkas game, but first I'm going to visit my old school friends," Zeke replied.

Xad and Quar both looked worried.

"You must be very careful, Zekelabraxis," said Quar. "Your Tragonian friends cannot discover the truth about Harris and Roxy."

As he struggled to eat the zilnit rod, Harris thought about how funny it was that now Zeke had to protect their secret, just as he had protected Zeke's on Earth.

"Don't worry," said Roxy. "We'll be careful."

THE NEXT DAY WAS HARRIS and Roxy's final day on Tragas.

Harris and Roxy were wearing their transformo-rings to look Tragonian. "I'm a little nervous about meeting your friends," Harris said to Zeke.

"Kind of like me on my first day at Jefferson Elementary School," said Zeke.

Harris thought about how he had treated Zeke when they first met. He felt bad for a moment.

"But then you met us!" Roxy said, smiling.

Zeke smiled back.

The school bus pulled up. Or at least the Tragonian version of the school bus. It was actually a large, floating glass tube, big enough to fit thirty kids. The outside of the tube changed colors as it glided to a stop.

The three kids stepped on. Harris expected the usual loud scene of kids fooling around. He was stunned to see each Tragonian kid in a transparent meditation pod, balanced upside down on the point of one of their tentacles, with all their eyes closed.

"What kind of school bus is this?" Harris asked.

"Shhh . . ." scolded the tube's operator.

"On the way to school, we meditate and prepare for learning," Zeke explained in a whisper.

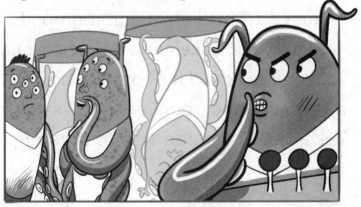

"Wow," Roxy said softly. "I bet some of our friends back on Earth would get better grades if they did this instead of trying to crack each other up."

"I don't think any of us can balance like that, though!" Harris said.

"Shhh . . ." the operator repeated.

A few minutes later, the tube glided to a stop in front of the school, which was shaped like a planet, complete with crisscrossing rings. The kids emerged from their meditation pods.

"Look, it's Zekelabraxis!" cried one Tragonian boy. The boy reached out a tentacle and touched elbows with Zeke, the Tragonian way of greeting.

"Xebtranic," said Zeke, "it is good to see you. I'd like you to meet a couple of new friends of mine. "This is Harris—agithran and Roxy-moltezix. They're from the other side of Tragas."

Zeke knew that his Earth friends' real names would arouse suspicion. Everyone on Tragas had long, complicated names.

Xebtranic extended his elbow toward Harris, who looked a bit stunned and confused. Roxy gently nudged Harris, who extended one of his tentacles.

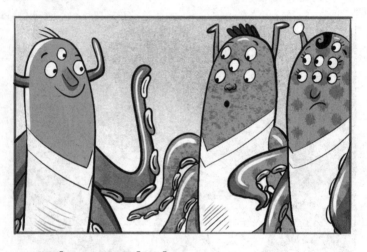

Zeke panicked.

Harris's body is just a mind projection illusion! He has no tentacle to touch. Xebtranic will find out that he's not really from Tragas.

Zeke quickly used his mind powers to push Harris back a step.

"Harrisagithran is a bit shy, but he's a nice kid," said Zeke, doing his best to cover for his friend.

Xebtranic extended an elbow toward Roxy. This time, Zeke mind-projected the feeling of elbows touching into Xebtranic's mind.

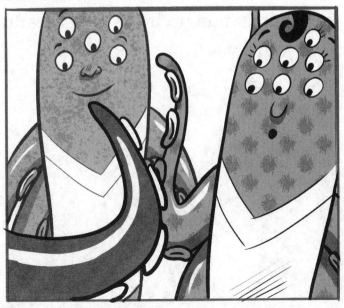

The kids were all off the tube and almost in the school building when Xebtranic realized that he had left behind his learning vid-pad. Seeing that Harris was the closest, Xebtranic called out: "Harrisagithran, can you send me my vid-pad? I'm too far away to get it myself."

He looked to Zeke, who whispered: "Put your hands up by your head and close your eyes."

Harris followed Zeke's instructions. To everyone watching, it appeared that two of Harris's tentacles moved up to his head and all five of his eyes had closed.

Zeke closed his eyes and secretly used his mind to reach into the tube, grab the vid-pad, and send it hurtling to Xebtranic.

"Thanks!" Xebtranic yelled, snatching the vid-pad out of the air. "Nice to meet you!"

As he watched his friends disappear into the school building, Zeke suddenly felt sad. As much as he hadn't wanted to leave Earth, now that he was home, he realized that he did miss his old life a little.

"Are you okay?" Roxy asked, noticing Zeke's expression.

"Tomorrow, we all blast off for Earth," Zeke said. "And I'll have to say goodbye to you and Harris all over again."

Or . . . will I? Zeke thought.

9 GOING BONKAS

THAT AFTERNOON, ZEKE, HARRIS, and Roxy walked into the Bonkas stadium. They were all excited about seeing a match. Sitting high up in the stands, the three friends looked out at the lush orange field.

"This is the same feeling I get when I step out and see a green baseball field on Earth," said Harris.

"Bonkas is similar to baseball," Zeke explained, "only instead of four bases on the field, there are ten sandpits."

"I see them," said Harris looking down at the field. "Weird."

"Not really," said Zeke. "Unlike baseball, Bonkas is played with ten balls at once. Each ball belongs to a certain sandpit. The hitter smacks the ten balls, then has to zoom around the entire field before the fielders can catch all ten balls and toss them into their corresponding sandpits."

Harris scratched his head.

"Watch," said Zeke.

The game began. Zeke rooted for the Slammers, his favorite team. Harris and Roxy cheered them on, too.

The first Slammers batter got up.

Holding all ten balls in his tentacles, the pitcher flung the balls toward the batter.

The batter whipped his bat around and drove each ball out into the field.

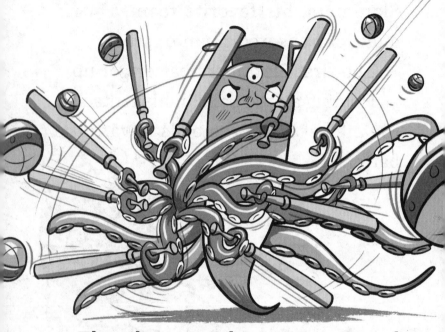

Then he started zooming around the edge of the field.

"This is really exciting!" said Roxy.

"Come on, run!" shouted Harris. "I mean, float . . . really fast!"

The fielders chased down the ten balls and then flung each of them toward the correct sandpits. The batter completed his circle of the field before the ten balls were in the pits, and scored a point for the Slammers.

The game continued, and the Slammers ended up winning.

"That was really fun," Roxy said as they left the stadium.

"Maybe we can try playing baseball with ten balls at a time," Harris joked.

"We have to hurry," said Zeke. "We're meeting my parents for dinner, and we don't want to be late."

The three friends met up with Zeke's parents at their favorite restaurant on Tragas.

"You know, I think I'm getting used to the food on Tragas," Roxy said, slurping down a gardash strand.

"Yeah, and if I forget that kreslars are actually slugs, they really don't taste too bad."

Zeke laughed. Then the conversation turned serious.

"We will blast off tomorrow just after the suns rise," Xad said.

"Suns?" Roxy asked.

"Yes, Tragas orbits three suns," Quar explained.

"Wow," said Roxy.

Xad continued. "The ship will be fully fueled by morning. I suggest you kids get a good night's sleep before our long journey back to Earth."

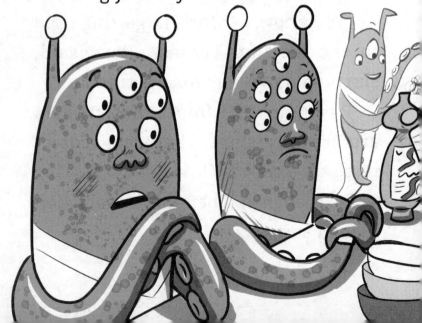

"Earth!" Harris exclaimed, spitting out the sip of Saurlic he had just taken. "Our parents! I forgot all about them."

"We've been missing for weeks!" said Roxy, panicking. "They must think that something terrible has happened to us. I feel awful putting them through that."

"What are we going to do?" asked Harris.

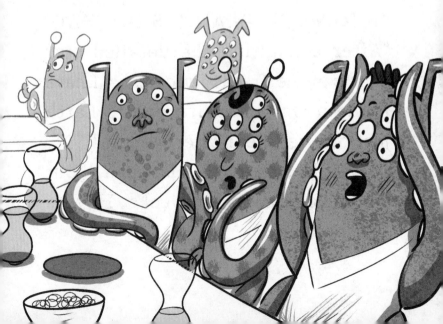

"I HAVE A PLAN," SAID XAD. "After consulting the detailed star charts at the Tragas Space Labs, I have found a way to return you to Earth just one half hour after we left."

Harris scratched his head. "But we've been gone for weeks. How is that possible?"

"Wormhole travel," Xad explained.
He pressed two tentacles to his head
and mind-projected a star field onto
the ceiling of the restaurant. In the
middle of the star-filled darkness, a
funnel-like cloud spun.

"By adjusting our return course and actually heading farther away from Earth, we can fly through this wormhole," Xad said. "Time and space act differently in wormholes. If all goes well, we should come out the other side of the wormhole very close to Earth and only half an hour after we blasted off from there weeks ago."

"Thinking about that makes my head hurt," said Roxy. "But I hope it works!"

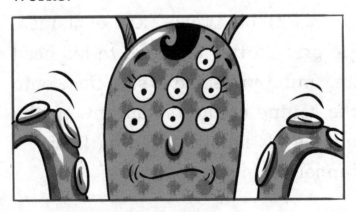

The next morning, everyone headed for the spaceport. Just before they boarded the spaceship, they watched the three suns of Tragas rise.

"Wow!" said Roxy. "What a sight!"

"You know, Zeke, I'm kind of sad to be leaving Tragas," said Harris. "There are so many cool things here, and we only got to check out a few of them."

"I'm glad we got to see your home," added Roxy.

"I'm glad you got to visit Tragas, too," says Zeke. "But I'm bummed that once we drop you off on Earth, I'll be coming back here without you."

Harris's mind raced as he and the others boarded the spaceship.

"What if we come up with a plan that keeps you and your parents on Earth?" Harris asked as he and Roxy took off their transformo-rings.

"Like what?" asked Zeke after he put on his translator glasses. "We tried to do that before, and failed."

"Well, now we've got this whole long trip back to Earth to figure something out," said Roxy.

"I guess we do," said Zeke, smiling.

"Strap in, everybody," said Quar.

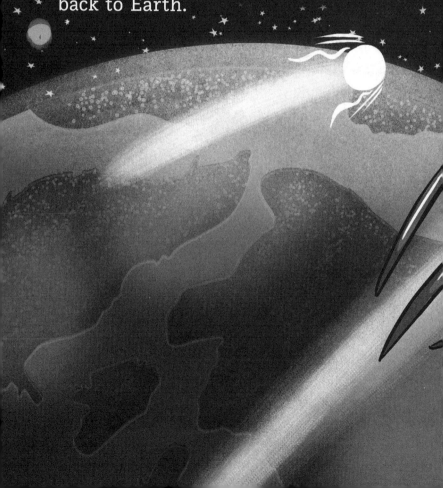

"We are ready for takeoff."

The spaceship started to rumble, and then it blasted off into the purple sky, zooming away from Tragas, and back to Earth.

READ ON FOR A SNEAK PEAK FROM THE FIRST BOOK IN THE **ISLE OF MISFITS SERIES!**

—— CHAPTER ONE ——

THE LONELIEST GARGOYLE

Gibbon the gargoyle lived atop the same castle all his life. Gargoyles were meant to protect the buildings they lived on. Sometimes, that meant protecting the people inside those buildings, too. That's what Gibbon was always taught.

But Gibbon couldn't stay still in one place *all* day. Sure, it was what he was *supposed* to do, but it was boring! So Gibbon found something new to do to pass the time: playing pranks on people as they walked by below.

And winter was his favorite season for pranks. Winter meant snowballs.

One snowy day, he saw a man in a suit hurrying by the castle. Gibbon quickly made a snowball in his hands. He held it over the edge and dropped it, watching as it hit the man right on the head.

The man jumped from the shock of the cold snow. A confused look crossed his face when he didn't see anyone around. Holding back laughter, Gibbon rolled another snowball and dropped it on the man. This time, the man yelped and ran off.

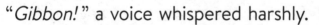

"*Gibbon!*" a voice whispered harshly.

He jumped and turned toward the gargoyle speaking to him. Elroy was the leader of the castle gargoyles and almost never broke his silence.

"That's enough," Elroy ordered. "You are too old to be playing pranks on the humans. You need to start taking your post seriously."

"But it's so boring!" Gibbon protested. "We just stand around all day. Even at night, we do nothing! What are we even defending the castle from anyway?"

Elroy did not move, but his eyes glared over at Gibbon. "You need to learn how to work with your team, Gibbon. Your slacking off only makes it harder for the rest of us."

With a sigh, Gibbon looked down at the street. He watched as a group of kids stopped below the castle. One of them picked up some snow and threw it at another. Instead of getting mad, the other kid started laughing and made his own snowball. In no time at all, the kids were in a full-fledged snowball fight!

That's what I want, Gibbon thought. For a very long time, Gibbon watched people's lives from the top of the castle. A lot of them had friends and family and fun, but Gibbon didn't really have any of that. The other gargoyles never wanted to play or laugh. They only wanted to watch the world as it went by.

Maybe if I can get Elroy to play, everyone else will loosen up! he thought.

Gibbon smiled. "Hey, Elroy. Catch me if you can! If you do, I'll sit still and guard the castle the rest of the day!"

With a laugh, Gibbon took off. He climbed down the side of the castle, then darted down an empty street.

Gibbon knew—he just *knew*—if Elroy played with him, he'd understand.

But when he stopped and looked back, he didn't see Elroy. His heart sank.

A. I. NEWTON always wanted to travel into space, visit another planet, and meet an alien. When that didn't work out, he decided to do the next best thing—write stories about aliens! The Alien Next Door series gives him a chance to imagine what it's like to hang out with an alien. And you can do the same—unless you're lucky enough to live next door to a real-life alien!

ANJAN SARKAR graduated from Manchester Metropolitan University with a degree in illustration. He worked as an illustrator and graphic designer before becoming a freelancer, where he now gets to work on all sorts of different illustration projects! He lives in Sheffield, England.

anjansarkar.co.uk

LOOK FOR MORE BOOKS IN
THE *ALIEN NEXT DOOR* SERIES!

Journey to some magical places, rock out, and find your inner superhero with these other chapter book series from **Little Bee Books**!

little bee books